I0765551

this Plot Gay edition is for

with lots of love

How to read this book

emotional support bird

This book has some hard words.

The first time you see a hard word

- the hard word is blue
- then you will see what the hard word means.

bold

not bold

Names are written in **bold**.

How to read this book

The pictures help you understand the words.

You can ask for help to read this story from

- a friend
- family
- or a support worker.

No farks

by **Casey Gray**

This is **Eddy** and their support bird **Fred**.

Eddy and **Fred**

DJ side by side.

Meet **DJ**

Judith Scott

The Mad Rapper

and **DJ**

Freeda Calmalot.

This is their

first song.

Hello queens.

I once said no to

The Mad Rapper.

I did not let

The Mad Rapper

have their mail.

My bum hole hurt.

I had to go back

into my cage.

Speed read.

Read a lot really fast.

Think.

Go back to school.

Learn about my

power over

The Mad Rapper.

Learn to respect **The Mad Rapper's** choices.

Not shit on them.

Now when I support

The Mad Rapper.

I have to do one

easy test.

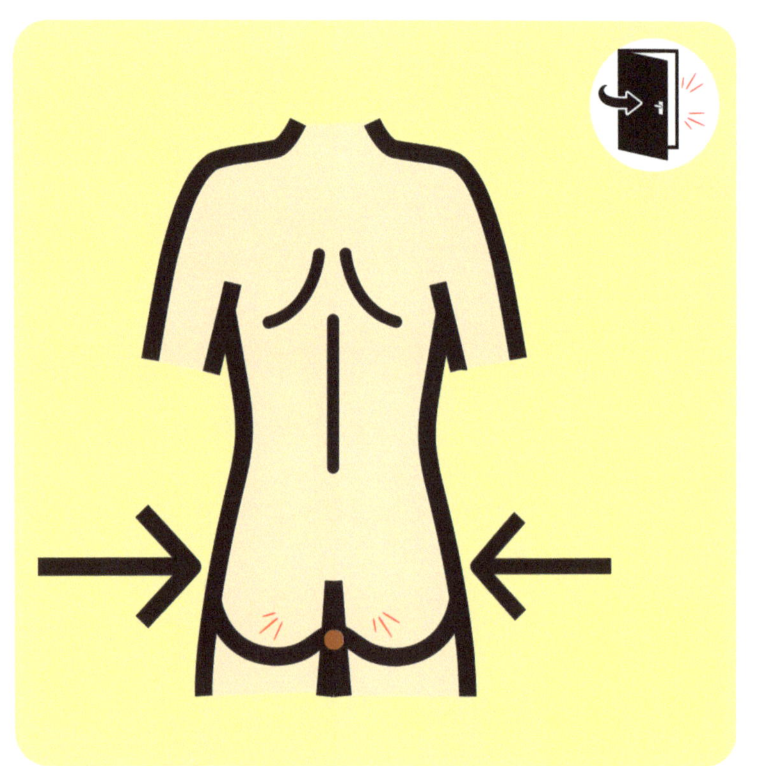

The Butt Clench Test.

A test to see if your bum hole closes.

To answer

one question.

Am I a

gate keeper?

A gate keeper

makes choices for

other people.

They can say

yes or no.

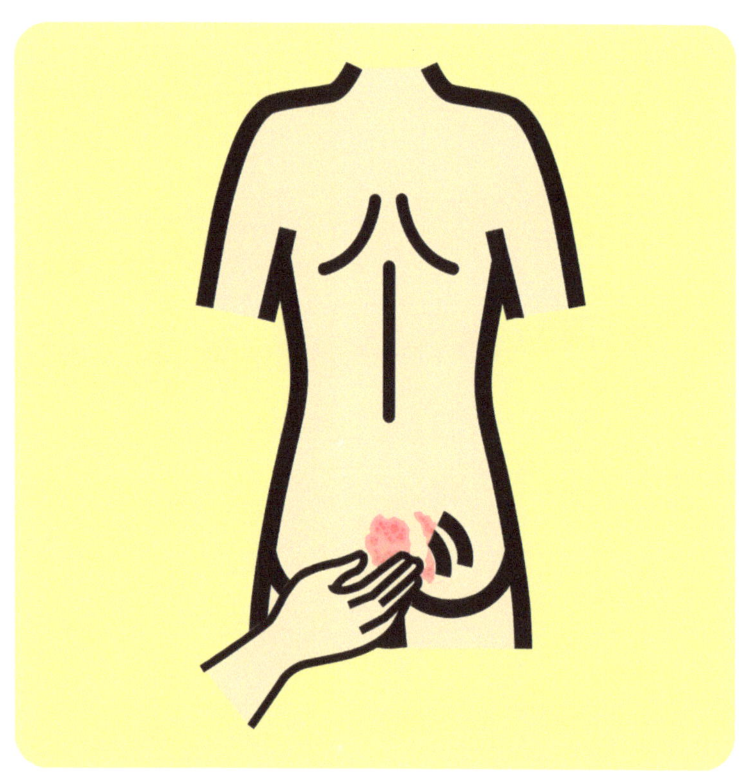

So if your bum

feels itchy.

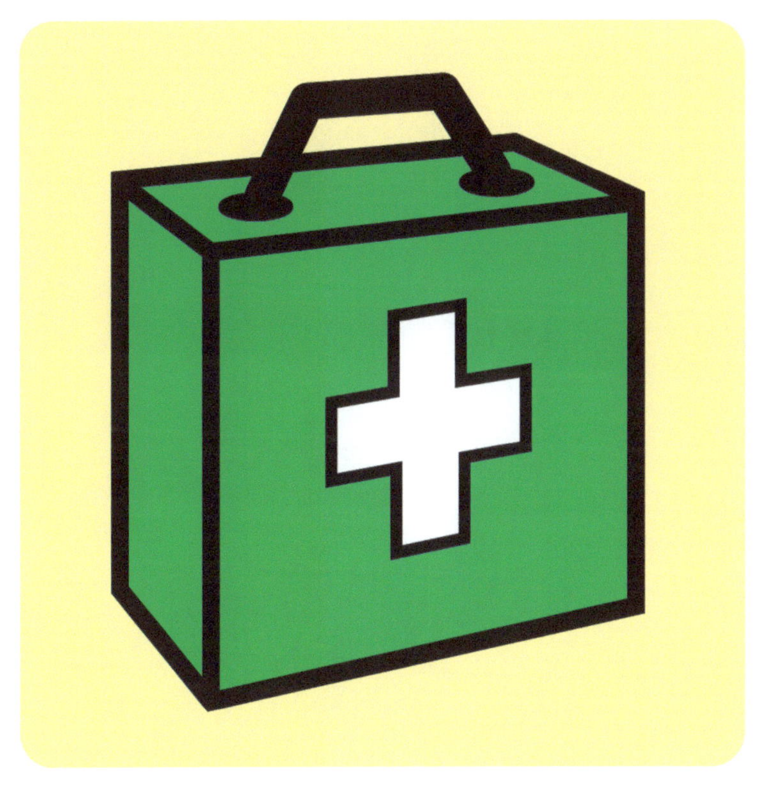

When you hear

the words

health and safety.

You are a

gate keeper.

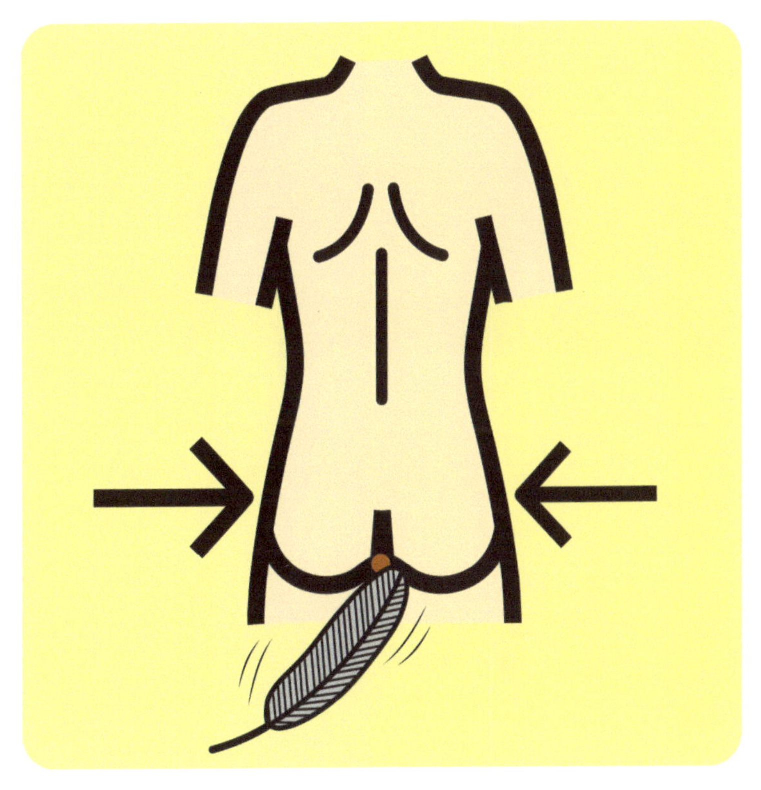

And if your

butt hole tickles.

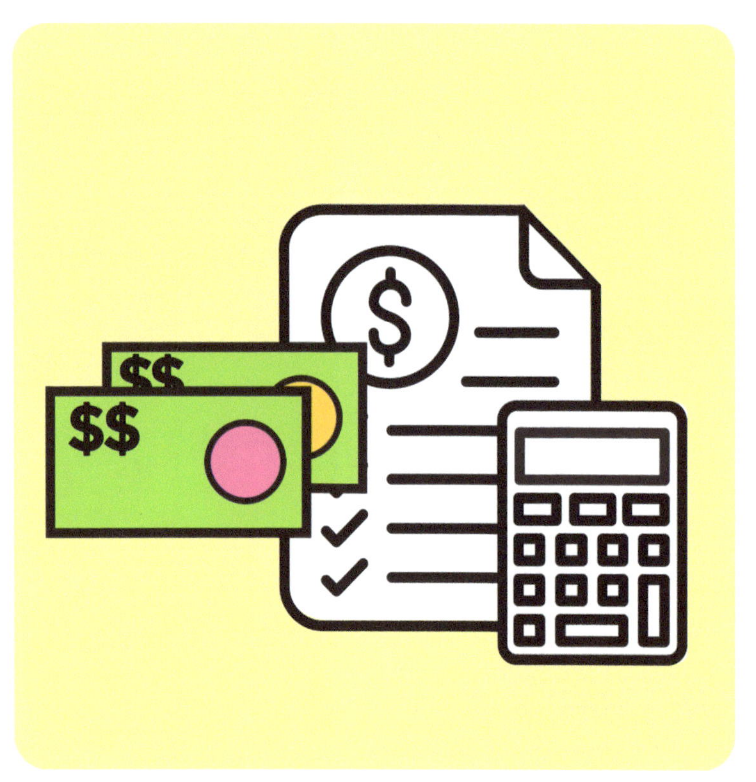

When you hear the word budget.

You are a

gate keeper.

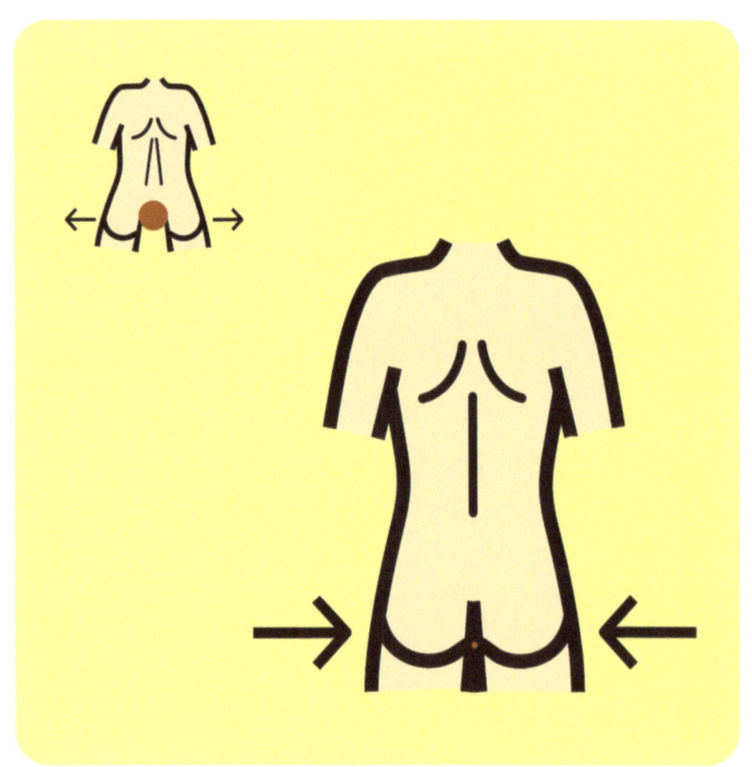

If your

butt hole closes.

When you hear
the words
sex or goals.

You are a

gate keeper.

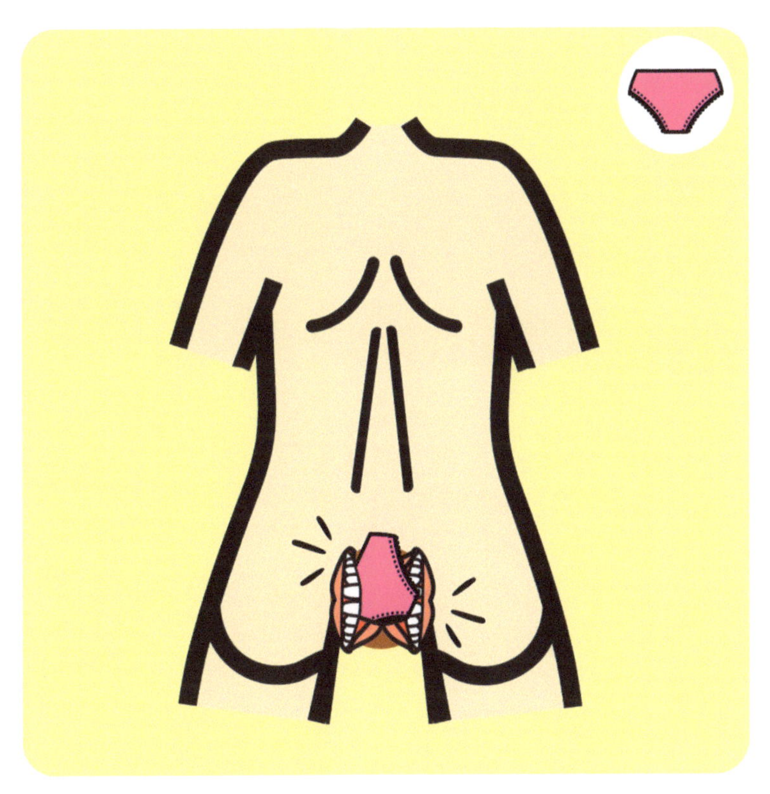

If your butt hole

eats your undies.

When you hear
the words.

Sex goals.

You are a

gate keeper.

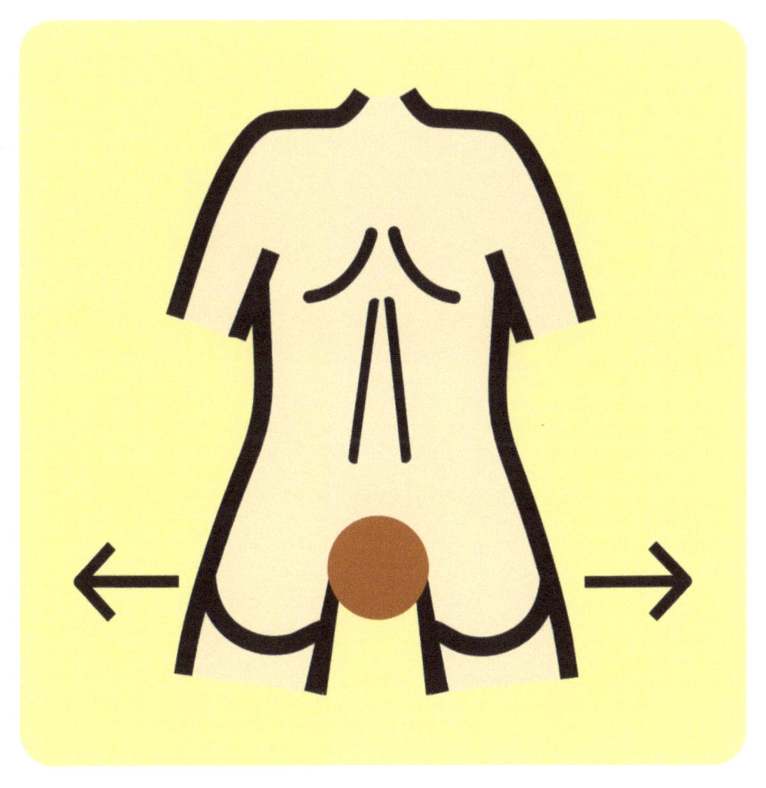

And if your butt

hole opens.

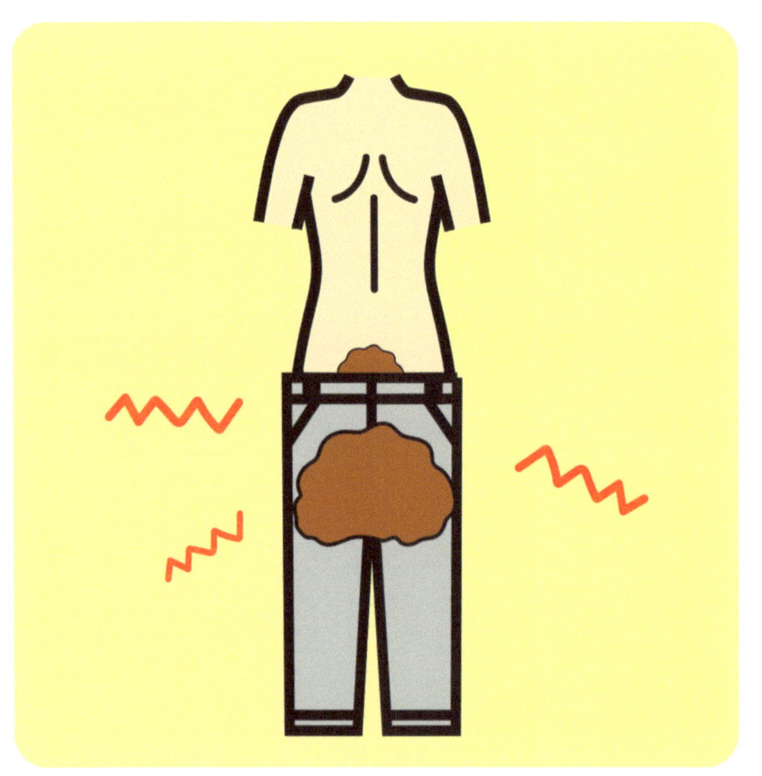

And you shit

your pants.

When someone yells.

Mum is on the phone

You are a

gate keeper.

If you are **Mum**.

We love you.

But you are also a

gate keeper.

And **The Mad Rapper** has a message for all of you.

We give no farks
about the forms
you use.

Unless they make

life good.

And we give no farks about the boxes you tick.

Unless they make

life good.

So think about

your power.

You can make

life good.

And remember...

Your butt

does not answer

to the system.

Your butt

answers to me.

A page to say thank you

Thank you **Cameron** from **Rainbow Rights** for helping me learn more about what a gate keeper means to adults with disability.

*"A gate keeper means they have someone controlling their life for them. They do not let them do anything. Not letting them have a partner or stepping in. Not letting them be active in the community or have choices or anything to say, or even sometimes people have to ask permission on what to do, where to go, what to eat and how to spend their money. No one wants this when they are over 18. No we don't." - **C. Bloomfield**, 2021.*

A page to say thank you

Thank you **Glitta Supernova** and **Juan** for creating a fun and inclusive place to live as well as giving artists like me a place to share our work.

Thank you **Fionn** and **Ben Drew** and all the other advocates who help make like good for everyone.

Thank you to my friends who helped me make this book better.

 There is strength in unity. Together our voices are loud. 

Printing information

Title: **No farks**

Author: **Casey Gray**

Published by **Books By ED**

Copyright © 2025 **Casey Gray, Books By ED**

Images copyright © 2025 **Casey Gray.** Any stock images are used under license.

Symbols from **Mulberry Symbols** https://mulberrysymbols.org/ Copyright 2018/19 **Steve Lee** - This work is licensed under the Creative Commons Attribution-ShareAlike 2.0 UK: England & Wales License.

ISBN: 978-0-6459693-6-8

Books By ED, Gosford NSW, Australia.

We recognise that this land was never ceded and pay respects to Elders past and present, and we extend that respect to all First Nations people.

All rights reserved. Set in Large Print minimum 14 pt. Poppins.

No part of this book may be reproduced or transmitted in any form or by any means, electronic or mechanical, including photocopying, recording, or by any information storage and retrieval system, without written permission from the author.

For more information https://www.byed.com.au/contact